A HAPPY ENDING BOOK ™

Tiggy and the Babysitter

by Jane Carruth   illustrated by Tony Hutchings

MODERN PUBLISHING

A Division of Unisystems, Inc.
NEW YORK, NEW YORK 10022
Printed in Belgium

"Come and look at my new doll house before we have something to drink," Tiggy cried, as soon as her best friend Tracy arrived one afternoon. "It's super!"

"I wish I had a doll house," sighed Tracy, after she had admired it. "I don't even have my favorite doll, Rosie. She is away being mended. And I won't have her tonight when Mrs. Prickles comes to babysit."

"What bad luck!" Tiggy exclaimed. "Mrs. Prickles doesn't even know any stories. She just sits and sits."

After Tracy had gone home, Tiggy's mother rushed into the room and told Tiggy to clean up. But Tiggy just stared at her. "What's the matter?" Mommy asked.
"You look funny with that towel around your head!" giggled Tiggy.
"Never mind how I look," Mommy said. "If you don't put your dolls away there won't be anyplace for Wanda to sit when she comes."

When Tiggy heard that Wanda was the new babysitter Mommy had found for tonight, she stamped her foot and burst into tears. "I don't want a dull old babysitter!" she screamed. Then she stormed out of the room.
Crash! Bang! Clatter! Down went Daddy's tea-tray as he caught her in his arms.

"Dear, oh dear!" Daddy cried. "What's all this! My little Tiggy is so upset!"

"She is being very silly," said Mommy.

"Then let's find out what all the fuss is about," said Daddy, as he made Tiggy sit between them.

"Wanda is Mrs. Prickles' younger sister," said Mommy.

"She is here on vacation from the big city where she teaches."

However, Tiggy didn't want to hear about Wanda. "I'm sure she will be just awful," she muttered, as she followed her mother upstairs. Mommy sat down in front of the mirror and began fixing her hair.

Then Daddy came in. "I think I'm bursting out of my new checkered shirt already," he groaned. "Perhaps I should wear an old one."

"Nonsense!" said Mommy. "The Mayor will expect you to look presentable. This is a very important meeting. We must stop that noisy factory from being built on our doorstep."

"Is that why you're going out?" asked Tiggy.

After Mommy had explained all over again about the importance of the meeting, Tiggy got into bed. Then the doorbell rang and soon there was Daddy standing at the bedroom door with Wanda. Tiggy stared. Wanda was really something! She had never seen anyone so neat and pretty. However, she wasn't going to show her surprise. She pulled the sheet over her face and pretended that she was falling asleep.

Wanda chuckled softly and said, "I know a story about a Princess who couldn't stay awake . . ."

"Tiggy won't be any trouble," said Mommy quickly. "I'll show you where things are in the kitchen. Then we'll leave. We're very grateful that you could come at such short notice."

Tiggy stayed very still until she heard the front door shut. Then she crept downstairs and into the kitchen. On the table was a basket of freshly washed sheets. Tiggy took the smallest and draped it over her head.

Wanda was too busy dancing to some music to notice her ghostly visitor right away. And Tiggy was so suprised to find her babysitter dancing, that she forgot to keep flapping her arms.

Before Tiggy had time to think what a ghost should do next, Wanda screamed out loud, "Help! A ghost!" Then she fell over backwards.

"Don't be scared!" cried Tiggy. "It's only me! I'm—I'm not a real ghost, you know. I-I just . . . well, I thought . . ."

"You thought you'd like to scare your babysitter," Wanda said cheerfully, pretending to recover.

"Well, sort of," Tiggy admitted, beginning to feel ashamed. "I-I didn't know you would be dancing. You see, Mrs. Prickles just sits and sits."

"I brought my own records with me," said Wanda. "And some very special storybooks for you to look at just in case you couldn't sleep."

Wanda helped Tiggy fold the sheet and put it back in the basket. Then she said, "Let's have some hot chocolate. After all, it's not every day a ghost comes to scare me!" Soon they were sitting at the table and talking like old friends. Tiggy could not believe that anyone as young as Wanda could have seen so many strange sights or done so many interesting things. "Did you really bring some books?" she asked at last.

"Of course I did," said Wanda. "Come and I'll show you. I use some of them in my class."

"Mrs. Prickles doesn't know any good stories," Tiggy confided, after she saw all the lovely, exciting books Wanda had brought.

"Well, she doesn't have much time for reading," explained Wanda. "She has to work so hard. Now, let's read the Princess story together."

Much sooner than she expected, Tiggy began to feel
sleepy. She rubbed her eyes and yawned.
Wanda finished the story. Then she took Tiggy up to bed.
''I think you will sleep now,'' she smiled. ''But I'll stay with
you until the Sandman comes to visit you.''
Then very sweetly and softly she began to sing Tiggy's
favorite lullaby.